Jack and
the Ghost

First published in 2009
by Wayland

This paperback edition published in 2010 by Wayland

Text copyright © Andy Blackford 2009
Illustration copyright © Marijke Van Veldhoven 2009

Wayland
338 Euston Road
London NW1 3BH

Wayland Australia
Level 17/207 Kent Street
Sydney, NSW 2000

Series Editor: Louise John
Cover design: Paul Cherrill
Design: D.R.ink
Consultant: Shirley Bickler

A CIP catalogue record for this book is available from the British Library.

ISBN 9780750258074 (hbk)
ISBN 9780750259590 (pbk)

Printed in China

Wayland is a division of Hachette Children's Books,
an Hachette UK Company

www.hachette.co.uk

Jack and the Ghost

Written by Andy Blackford
Illustrated by Marijke Van Veldhoven

WAYLAND

Jack was on holiday. He was staying in a cottage with his mum and dad.

The cottage was in a dark wood. It was quite spooky.

Before he went to sleep, Jack
read a book called **The
Haunted House**. It was all
about ghosts.

In the middle of the night there was a loud bump. It sounded as if someone was walking around downstairs.

Jack's dad went to have a look, but nobody was there.

In the morning, Jack's mum said, "I wonder what was making all that noise last night?"

"Maybe it was a ghost,"
said Jack.

His dad laughed. "There are no such things as ghosts, Jack. It was probably a cat or the hot water pipes."

12

14

Later, Jack met the gho[st] [on]
the stairs. "Hello," he sa[id].
"I'm Jack. Who are you[?"]

"I'm Frank," replied the ghost. "This is my house. I've lived here for three hundred years."

"You were making a lot of noise last night," Jack told him. "You woke everybody up."

"Sorry," said Frank. "I was in a bad mood. I'm fed up because nobody is scared of me any more."

17

"Wait!" smiled Jack. "I've got an idea!"

That night, Frank juggled with plates.

Dad's tea flew across the room.

Frank blew out the fire.

He made the lights go out.
Then he let the bats in!

Soon, Jack's mum and dad really did believe in ghosts.

Then Frank said, "Hello!"

Mum and Dad shook Frank's hand, and soon they were not scared of him at all.

Jack showed Frank **The Haunted House**.

Frank liked it a lot. "Ghosts don't read ghost stories," he said. "We read people stories instead. They're really spooky!"

The next day, it was time to
go home. Jack and his mum
and dad packed their bags.

"Goodbye," said Frank. "I'll miss you!"

At the last minute, Jack ran back to write in the visitors' book.

"We had a good time. The beds are nice and soft. But watch out for the REALLY scary ghost!"

START READING is a series of highly enjoyable books for beginner readers. **The books have been carefully graded to match the Book Bands widely used in schools.** This enables readers to be sure they choose books that match their own reading ability.

Look out for the Band colour on the book in our Start Reading logo.

The Bands are:

Pink Band 1

Red Band 2

Yellow Band 3

Blue Band 4

Green Band 5

Orange Band 6

Turquoise Band 7

Purple Band 8

Gold Band 9

START READING books can be read independently or shared with an adult. They promote the enjoyment of reading through satisfying stories supported by fun illustrations.

Andy Blackford used to play guitar in a rock band. Besides books, he writes about running and scuba diving. He has run across the Sahara Desert and dived with tiger sharks. He lives in the country with his wife and daughter, a friendly collie dog and a grumpy cat.

Marijke Van Veldhoven loves to make people laugh. At school she liked drawing cartoons of her friends and teachers that had everyone in hysterics! She lives happily in the Netherlands with her dog and two cats and enjoys long walks.